CRANBERRY
A New Baby in Cranberryport

Wende and *Harry Devlin*

ALADDIN BOOKS
Macmillan Publishing Company
New York
Maxwell Macmillan Canada
Toronto
Maxwell Macmillan International
New York   Oxford   Singapore   Sydney

Aladdin Books
Macmillan Publishing Company
866 Third Avenue
New York, NY 10022

Maxwell Macmillan Canada, Inc.
1200 Eglinton Avenue East
Suite 200
Don Mills, Ontario M3C 3N1

Macmillan Publishing Company is part of the Maxwell Communication Group of Companies.
First Aladdin Books edition 1994
Printed in the United States of America
10 9 8 7 6 5 4 3 2 1
The text of this book is set in 14 pt Stempel Shadow.

Library of Congress Cataloging-in-Publication Data
Devlin, Wende.
    A new baby in Cranberryport / Wende and Harry Devlin. — 1st Aladdin Books ed.
        p.   cm.—(Tales from Cranberryport)
    Summary: When her mother has a new baby, Annie fears everyone has forgotten about her, but
Grandmother and Mr. Whiskers help her remember that she is loved as well.
    ISBN 0-689-71780-6
    [1. Babies—Fiction. 2. Brothers and sisters—Fiction.] I. Devlin, Harry.   II. Title.
III. Series: Devlin, Wende.   Tales from Cranberryport.
PZ7.D49875Ne   1994
[E]—dc20   93-45819

For Annabelle Devlin

Exciting news in Cranberryport!

Grandmother and Maggie's next-door neighbors, Annie's parents, were going to have a baby.

"A baby is a wondrous thing," Annie's mother said, sharing her happy thoughts with Annie and Maggie.

"Will it be a boy or a girl?" Annie wondered.

"Either would be perfect." Everyone agreed on that.

    And now, there were so many things to be done. They painted the nursery soft yellow, bought clothes and a crib for the baby, and found a rocking chair for Annie's mother. Annie even helped paint Humpty Dumpty on the nursery wall.

    Weeks passed, and all was ready. The baby would be here any day.

Grandmother had insisted on one last party for Annie's mother—where everyone would come with a present for the new baby. Today was the day and Grandmother's guests would be here any minute. She bustled about, putting out linen napkins and silver that didn't quite match. Never mind—the house looked beautiful with pitchers of lilacs everywhere.

Mr. Whiskers, an old friend and neighbor, knocked
at grandmother's back door.

"Suffering codfish! Are you sure no men are
allowed?" he asked Grandmother. "Look at this dandy
new lobster trap I have for the baby."

"Sorry," said Grandmother as she waved him off.
He grumbled his way back home.

It was a happy party at Grandmother's. Annie's mother was showered with presents—tiny sweaters, nightgowns, soft-colored blankets, and toys. She was grateful.

"*Now* we are ready for the new baby," said Grandmother. She waved good-bye to her guests.

Suddenly Annie's mother caught her breath and sat down.

"The baby! Grandmother, I think I should get to the hospital." Grandmother ran for the phone. Annie's father wasn't in his office, but they would send him directly to the hospital as soon as he returned.

How to get Annie's mother to the hospital?

Mr. Whiskers! That's how! thought Grandmother.

They were soon on their way in Mr. Whiskers's dusty truck.

Grandmother tugged on Mr. Whiskers's coat. "You made it to our party after all."

Mr. Whiskers smiled through his whiskers.

The news came the next morning. Annie jumped
up and down with excitement.

"Maggie, Maggie, Mother's fine and Jamie's here.
We are going to have such fun with him." Maggie and
Annie made happy plans.

Annie's mother and new baby brother came home soon. But Annie found she wasn't quite ready for *all* the changes. Mother was busy with the baby; Father washed all the clothes and helped cook dinner. Somehow there wasn't a minute to play. What happened to all of Annie's happy summer plans?

When Annie did spend a weekend with Maggie and Grandmother, she was very tired.

She dropped her suitcase on the porch with a crash.

"Grandmother," she said in a burst, "I am so happy to be here. Do you know how much new babies cry? No one has time to play. Mother tends to the baby all day—and with 'Isn't he sweet in his little lace hat'—they've forgotten all about *me*!"

"Suffering codfish." Mr. Whiskers felt sorry for
Annie. "It must be hard when someone new squeezes
into the nest and gets all the attention."

"It just takes a little time," encouraged Grandmother. "Of course, if you move over just a little, that someone new *could* become your best friend."

Annie just sighed.

But over the weekend at Grandmother's, thoughts of home slipped into her mind—Jamie's smile, mother's love, father's joking kindness. On Sunday, after Annie thanked Maggie and Grandmother for the visit, she ran home and up the front stairs two at a time. Home!

Annie's mother hugged her at the front door.
"Oh, how we have missed you, Annie. Can't we
spend more time together—just you and me? You are
my baby too, you know!"

They missed me, thought Annie.

Where was sweet Jamie?
"Could I take the baby to visit Mr. Whiskers today—
he's never seen him in his little lace hat?"

Annie laughed at herself—she realized she had just moved over in the nest and she felt fine.

"Isn't a baby a wondrous thing?"